Butterfly Kids Co

+Fun Facts for Kids to Read about Butterflies

Children Activity Book for Girls & Boys Age 4-8, with 30 Super Fun Coloring Pages of Butterflies in Lots of Fun Actions!

A butterfly lover? How much do you know about how the butterfly turns into a beautiful winged creature? Well, here's how. The butterfly starts its life as an egg, laid on a leaf. The caterpillar (larva) then hatches from the egg and starts eating flowers and leaves. As it grows, the caterpillar loses skin and increases its size turning into a chrysalis, and finally a beautiful adult butterfly!

You can smell your feet but can you taste with it?! Eww! But in the butterfly world, they can easily say if a plant is tasty or not by simply standing on it! This is also used to find the right plant to lay its eggs. Now don't try standing on your food!

Butterflies are magnificent creatures with unique beautiful patterns on their wings but if you look close enough, butterfly wings are actually clear! The tiny scales on their wings reflect the various patterns and colours we see on their wings. Isn't nature amazing?!

There are lots of insects around the world and they have all been divided into different classes to better identify them. Butterflies belong to the class called Lepidoptera and why? Because of their scaly wings!

How far would you go to avoid the winter chills? Both birds and butterflies can fly but only monarch butterflies travel over 2500 miles every winter!

A group of birds is a flock, but
what is a group of butterflies?
A bunch of butterflies together is
called a flutter and that's also
what you call when a butterfly
flaps its wings!

You may have seen dog poo and bird droppings but have you spotted butterfly droppings? Hardly, because many butterflies don't excrete their waste! Everything they eat is used by the body for energy and hardly anything is left out!

If you see butterflies in a mud puddle, it's not because it's fun jumping into them like we do but did you know that male butterflies actually drink from mud puddles?! They do this to get the extra amount of nutrients absent in flowers. This is also called puddling!

Guess who can compete
with a horse?
A butterfly!
Yes, Skipper butterflies can fly up
to 37 miles per hour and can even
outrun a horse!

Careful! Butterflies can turn into
bloodthirsty beasts!
Some butterflies will drink the
blood from your open wounds!
They are not so sweet after all!

Did you know that butterflies
go to clubs?!
Yes, they are way more
cool than you think!
A group of butterflies puddling
together at wet soil areas
extracting minerals is called a
"puddle club".

Who's munching food in your garden? It's the caterpillars! Sometimes, if you listen real close, you can actually hear a bunch of caterpillars munching away the leaves!

If you've read the Very Hungry Caterpillar, you'd know how hungry a caterpillar can get and it's true! As soon as the caterpillar hatches from its cocoon, it usually eats the shell of the cocoon itself.

Monarch butterflies are gorgeous in colour but definitely poisonous in nature! Monarch butterflies have beautiful contrasting colours that warn its predators of its toxicity. Monarch butterflies are considered venomous because they love eating the poisonous milkweed plant!

Seeds and fruits are not the greatest choice to feed your butterfly friends.
In fact, butterflies don't have teeth; they have a liquid diet and only feed on liquids and cannot chew solid food.

All this time, you thought butterflies drink sap from flowers?

Wrong!

Butterflies have a long tube-like tongue called a proboscis though which they suck in the food, instead of drinking it!

Where do you think the butterfly has
its ears? Certainly not on the sides
of its head but on its wings!
Some butterflies have ears on their
wings which help them distinguish
various sounds from other birds.
Next time you talk to a butterfly,
talk to the wing!

Despite their natural beauty, butterflies have a very small lifespan. Small butterflies we find in the garden live only up to about one week, while some last for a couple of months.

It is always fun to look at the varying sizes of butterflies! The largest butterfly ever found is Queen Alexandra's Birdwing with a wing extending up to 12 inches! while the smallest is the Western Pygmy with a wing of only 0.75 inches wide.

Did you know that a butterfly
can't fly if they're cold?
Butterflies are cold blooded
insects and if the temperature
falls too low, they cannot move.
Butterflies sure need to warm up
before taking off!

Butterflies don't have lungs but where do they breathe from?! Butterflies have small openings in their stomachs called spiracles which help them breathe.

How gross would it be if our bones stuck out from our bodies?!
We'd all look like zombies!
But butterflies have exoskeletons and they look gorgeous!
Butterflies have skeletons outside the bodies protecting them while also keeping them well hydrated.

Don't forget to come close
or the butterfly won't be able
to see you properly!
Butterflies can only see objects
within 10 to 20 feet distance.
However they can also see
ultraviolet rays that are invisible
to the human eye!

Butterflies are way more cunning than you think! It's interesting to know that some butterflies have false heads at the back of their wings, so that when predators attack, they would bite off the false head leaving the true one untouched!

Have you ever had
a nice babysitter while your
mommy is out?
Well, caterpillars have ant
babysitters!
Mommy butterflies rely on ants
to take care of their babies and
the ants protect these
caterpillars from parasites.
In return, the caterpillars provide
nutrients while some may even
feed on the ant larvae! So much
for babysitting!

Butterflies are
everywhere you go!
Can there be any place without
butterflies around?
Yes, it's Antarctica!

Here's a tip if you're making
a butterfly garden!
Butterflies, as much as
they're beautiful, can be
very picky about where they
lay their eggs.
Some butterflies have
specific plants on which
they lay eggs.

Did you know that
there are almost
17500 different
butterfly species
around the world?!
No wonder you hardly
see the same butterfly
twice!

Is that a butterfly or a moth?
How can you know?!
Butterflies have long, smooth antennae rounded on the ends, whereas most moths have thick, feathery antennae. Moths also have larger, fuzzier bodies than butterflies. Even when they're resting, butterflies raise their wings up against each other while moths flatten their wings out.

Hi there!

It's me, Jackie D. Fluffy!

I hope you like this book like I do.

What's the next animal you want to color??

Let me know by writing a review on

www.amazon.com

Sure! It will be fun and useful!

With much thanks and love,

Jackie D. Fluffy

Made in the USA
Las Vegas, NV
26 May 2021

23665776R10035